The Adventures of BERT

ALLAN AHLBERG & RAYMOND BRIGGS

PUFFIN BOOKS

PUFFIN BOOKS

Published by the Penguin Group
Penguin Books Ltd, 80 Strand, London WC2R 0RL, England
Penguin Putnam Inc., 375 Hudson Street, New York, New York 10014, USA
Penguin Books Australia Ltd, 250 Camberwell Road, Camberwell, Victoria 3124, Australia
Penguin Books Canada Ltd, 10 Alcorn Avenue, Toronto, Ontario, Canada M4V 3B2
Penguin Books India (P) Ltd, 11 Community Centre, Panchsheel Park, New Delhi – 110 017, India
Penguin Books (NZ) Ltd, Cnr Rosedale and Airborne Roads, Albany, Auckland, New Zealand
Penguin Books (South Africa) (Pty) Ltd, 24 Sturdee Avenue, Rosebank 2196, South Africa

Penguin Books Ltd, Registered Offices: 80 Strand, London WC2R 0RL, England

www.penguin.com

First published by Viking 2001
Published in Puffin Books 2002
1 3 5 7 9 10 8 6 4 2

Set in Bembo

Made and printed in Italy by Printer Trento Srl

British Library Cataloguing in Publication Data
A CIP catalogue record for this book is available from the British Library

ISBN 0-140-56754-2

CHAPTER ONE

Bert

Meet Bert.
This is him.
Say hallo to Bert.

Meet Mrs Bert.
This is her.
Say hallo to her
as well.

Meet Baby Bert.
Don't say hallo to him.
He is fast asleep.

Shh!
Turn the page . . . quietly.

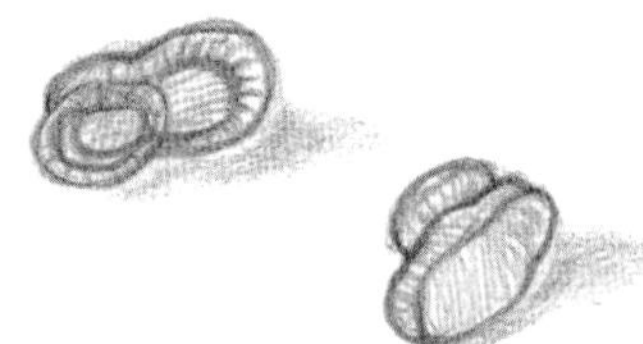

Oh no!
Now look what you've done.

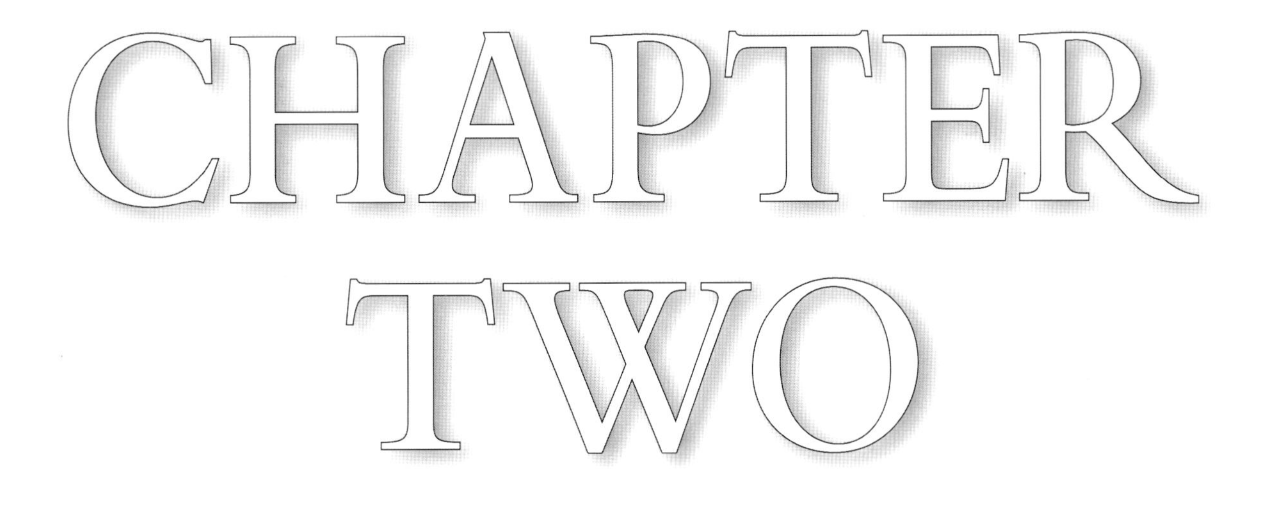

Bert and the Shirt

One day Bert has
an adventure with a shirt.

Here is the shirt.
Do you like it?

Bert puts
the shirt on.
It gets stuck
over his head.

He falls downstairs.

He rolls into the street.

He rolls into a lorry.

He ends up in Scotland.

Poor Bert!

CHAPTER THREE

Bert and the Sausage

The next day Bert has
an adventure with a sausage.

Bert is out shopping.
He sees a sausage in the street.

Bert runs off.

The sausage chases him.

Bert falls over.

Bert bangs his nose.

But it is only a man in a sausage suit,
selling sausages.
The sausage man helps Bert to his feet.
He gives him his hat back
. . . and a free sausage.

Lucky Bert!

Bert and the Cardboard Box

The *next* day Bert has
an adventure with a cardboard box.

Bert is walking by the river.
He sees a cardboard box go floating by.
There it is – look!

The box is big and brown
. . . and *barking*.

Bert dives in
to rescue the box.

Then he remembers –
he can't swim.

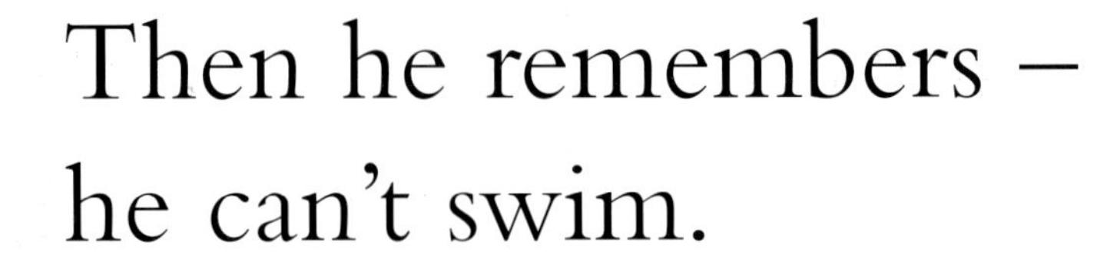

Bert splashes!

Bert shouts!

Bert sinks!

Bert . . . stands up.

The water is not as deep as he thought.

Bert lies on the bank.

A *puppy* creeps out of the box.

He licks Bert's face.

Bert is his hero.

Brave Bert!

CHAPTER FIVE

Goodnight, Bert!

It is bedtime now.
Bert is in his pyjamas.
Say goodnight to Bert.

Goodnight!

Mrs Bert is in her pyjamas.
Say goodnight to her as well.

Goodnight!

Baby Bert
is in his cot.
Don't say goodnight
to him.
Don't make a sound.

Shh!
Turn the page
very, very . . . quietly.

Oh no!
You've done it again!

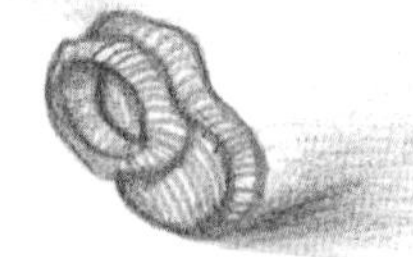

The End